The
Railway Rabbits

Wisher and the Noisy Crows

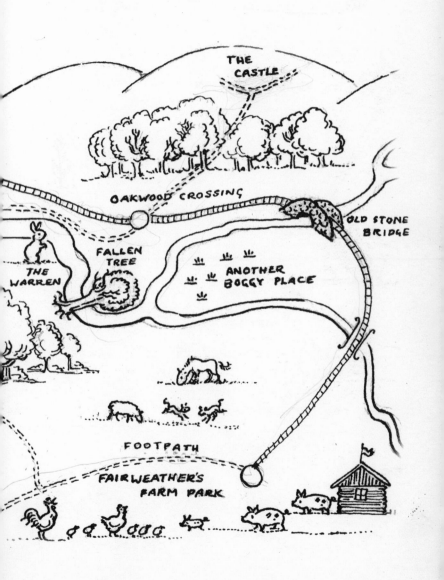

Trouble
in the
Crows'
Nest
1

One cold morning, Barley and
Mellow Longears were in the meadow
keeping an eye on their five young
rabbits – Bramble, Bracken, Berry, Fern
and Wisher.

"It's been a long winter," said Barley.

"Yes," said Mellow. "But it's nearly
over. Look. There are snowdrops in the
hedgerow. Spring isn't far away."

"I can't wait!" said Barley. "Spring is
my favourite time of year."

They listened to
the young rabbits' chatter.

"Let's play Hop-Back," said Bramble.
He had thick, black fur, but his paws felt
cold on the frosty grass.

Bracken and Berry were chasing
each other.

"Hey, you two!" said
Bramble. "Bend your backs.
I'll go first. Ready, Fern?
Ready, Wisher? Come on,
you're as slow as snails!"

"Why do we always
have to do what you say?"
said Berry. He had reddish-
brown fur, red as a rosehip. But he liked
playing Hop-Back and got ready to play.

"Because I'm the biggest," said
Bramble cheerfully.

"And the bossiest!" said Wisher.

Her silvery-white coat shone in the wintry sunshine.

"I think it's a good idea," said Bracken. He always tried to please Bramble. Gingery-brown Bracken placed himself three hops' distance from Berry and waited.

Fern gave her soft, grey fur a shake.

"Let's stop talking and start!" she said.

"Right," said Bramble. "Here I come!"

"Aren't we lucky, Barley Longears?" said Mellow. "We have five beautiful, healthy young rabbits."

Barley nodded. He looked towards the River Ripple and to the wooded hills beyond.

"This is a wonderful valley," he said. "I can't imagine living anywhere else."

"The best a rabbit could wish for!" said Mellow. Then she gave a little sigh. "I suppose, when Bramble, Bracken, Berry, Fern and Wisher are older, they will want to leave home, like we did. Just think, Barley, one day, our children will have families of their own."

"True," said Barley. "But until then, we'll do our best to keep them safe."

"We've taught them to take care up-burrow," said Mellow. "Sensible rabbits have careful habits!"

Barley glanced nervously at the telegraph pole where their number one enemy, Burdock the buzzard, often perched, waiting to catch a rabbit. To Barley's relief, the bird was nowhere to be seen.

"Burdock must be hunting somewhere else this morning," he said. "But we must be careful. I saw a fox about yesterday. He looked very hungry."

"Which reminds me," said Mellow. "I'm hungry too! Let's look for something to eat."

Wisher soon grew tired of playing Hop-Back, and she wandered off to be by herself. No one took any notice. They were used to Wisher's strange ways. She was a little different from the others, with her special gift of knowing things before they happened. Even Wisher didn't really understand how it worked. It was just something she was born with, a power she had inherited from her great-great eldermarr, Meadow Silvercoat.

As Wisher passed a prickly gorse bush, she felt the ground move. A small mound of earth appeared, shortly followed by another, and another.

"My friend, Parsley Mole, makes hills like these," she said. "I wonder if it's him?"

She didn't have to wait long to find out. Suddenly, an animal with large front paws and a whiskery snout popped out of a hole.

"Hello, Parsley!" said Wisher. "I hoped it was you."

"Good to see you, Wisher!" said Parsley, brushing dirt from his silky black coat.

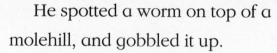

He spotted a worm on top of a molehill, and gobbled it up.

"Mmmm!" said Parsley.

"Yuck!" said Wisher.

Just then, they saw some crows flying towards the big oak.

Caw-caw-caw! cried the crows.

Wisher remembered Craggs and Clary Crow lived there. A few mintues later, they heard a terrible fuss.

Caw-caw-caw! Caw-caw-caw!

"Noisy birds!" said Parsley.

"They sound upset," said Wisher. "Let's see what's the matter."

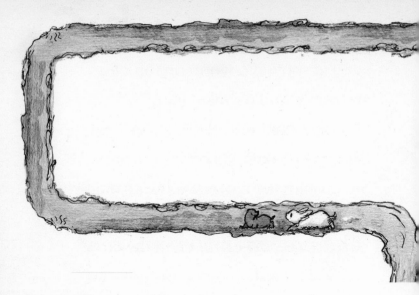

"Okay," said Parsley. "Come with me. It's quicker by tunnel!"

Parsley's passage was smaller than a rabbit burrow, but Wisher was just the right size to fit inside.

She followed him down a hole and along a twisty tunnel. Parsley knew his way around like the back of his paw. Suddenly, he stopped and sniffed.

"We're here," he said. "I can smell it!"

"You're very clever," said Wisher.

"Up we go!" said Parsley.

They climbed over tree roots, ran up a short slope and came out of a hole. The noise from the crows was deafening.

Caw-caw-caw! Caw-caw-caw!

Wisher looked up into the tree. Perched in the branches she could see large birds with blue-black feathers, all talking their beaks off. Craggs and Clary spotted her, and flew down with two of their friends.

The new crows introduced themselves:

"I'm Chuff," said one.

"I'm Chaff," said the other.

"Hello," said Wisher.

"Hi!" said Parsley.

"Chuff and Chaff have just come from Oak Wood," said Clary.

"They've had a fright," said Craggs.

"Oh, dear!" said Wisher. "What happened?"

"People-folk," said Chuff. "They're cutting trees."

"With a big machine," said Chaff.

Wisher and Parsley were surprised.

"People-folk?" they said together.

"We thought you might know something, Wisher," said Craggs.
"I remembered about your funny ears. Your special powers . . ."

"Special powers?" said Chuff.

"Cool!" said Chaff.

Wisher hated being the centre of attention. "It's something I was born with," she said.

"Usually, when something is about to
happen, my ears tingle and I hear a
voice inside my head. But not this time. I
have no idea what people-folk are doing
in Oak Wood."

"What if they cut all the trees?"
said Chaff.

"Don't!" said Chuff. "Oak Wood is our
home. I want to go back."

"I know how you feel," said Clary.
"Our old nest was destroyed by fire."

"That was when campers set light to the wood at the Farm Park," said Craggs. "Caw! You wouldn't believe how stupid some people-folk can be."

"Parsley and I were there," said Wisher. "It was very frightening."

"Hm!" said Clary. "People-folk had better not come here. Spring is coming. We're getting our nest ready for a family."

Wisher thought of her friend, Blinker Badger, and his family. They lived in Oak Wood. Then she thought of Marr and Parr and everyone at home.

"Oh, Clary!" she said. "Do you think people-folk will come?"

Clary shook her head.

"Who can say what they'll do, Wisher," she said.

"People-folk do as they please," said Craggs.

"We'll keep our ears and eyes open," said Chuff.

"If we hear anything, we'll tell you," said Chaff. "Unless . . ."

"What?" said Wisher.

"I was thinking about your special powers," he said. "Maybe you'll know before us?"

"Maybe," said Wisher, wondering why her ears hadn't warned her already if something bad was about to happen.

They all said goodbye, and Wisher hurried home to tell everyone the news.

Alarm
Bells
2

"People-folk in Oak Wood?" said Barley.

"Yes," said Wisher. "Some crows have lost their homes."

"Oh, buttercups!" said Barley. "People-folk will be taking over our burrows before we know it."

"Wriggly worms!" said Bramble.

"Slugs and snails!" said Bracken.

"Creeping caterpillars!" said Berry.

Fern looked about nervously, as if she expected to see people-folk marching across the meadow at any minute.

"When will they come, Parr?" she said. "I don't want to leave home. Where will we go? What if we're caught? People-folk eat rabbits, don't they? We'll be put in a pie. We're doomed FOR EVER!"

Mellow tried to calm everyone down. "We don't know anything of the sort, Fern," she said. "It's bad news, but if we're sensible . . ."

At that moment, Blinker Badger came along. He had taken his usual path through a specially made tunnel, which went under the Red Dragon's tracks, then across the river to the meadow where the Longears rabbits lived. Today, Blinker had brought one of his cubs.

"This is Briar," he said.

The rabbits introduced themselves.

"I'm Barley."

"I'm Mellow."

"I'm Bramble."

"I'm Bracken."

"I'm Berry."

"I'm Fern."

"And I'm Wisher!"

Briar stayed close to Blinker. The cub looked upset. Berry pulled a funny face to cheer him up, and Briar smiled.

"That's better, Briar!" said Blinker. Then to the rabbits: "I don't know if you've heard? There are people-folk in Oak Wood cutting trees. We're all very worried."

"They were making a lot of noise," said Briar. "Like this.

Buz-z-z-z-z-z-z-z-z!

The tree went *CRA-A-A-CK!*"

"It fell near our sett," said Blinker.

"Some crows told me they'd lost their homes," said Wisher.

"How dreadful!" said Blinker.

"Nothing would surprise me about people-folk," said Barley. "Not after my experience."

"What happened?" said Blinker.

"Didn't I tell you?" said Barley. "Not long ago I found myself at the Farm Park. Hazel Heron took me there by mistake. But that's another story! People-folk were holding a Pet Show. They thought I was one of the pets!"

Blinker looked puzzled. "Pets?" he said.

"Animals who live with people-folk," said Barley. "Like dogs and . . . rabbits! I was put in a cage with some pet rabbits, but I managed to get away."

Wisher remembered this story. Her parr had been very brave. He'd saved her from Burdock the buzzard and had fallen in the river. Then Hazel Heron had flown off with him. "It was the day of the Duck Race," she told Blinker.

"That's right," said Barley. "Which reminds me. On my way home, I saw people-folk putting ducks in a box!"

Blinker gasped.

"Whatever next?" he said. "My dear old friend, you had a lucky escape."

"Yes," said Barley. "So you see, I have a good reason not to trust people-folk. You never know what they're up to. From now on, we must all take extra care."

"I agree," said Blinker. "Our lives depend upon it!"

When Blinker and Briar went
home, Barley sat on his tree
stump to keep watch. Mellow
stayed close to the burrow. She
wasn't sure what she'd do if
any people-folk came, but
she hoped she'd put up a
good fight.

Bramble, Bracken,
Berry, Fern and Wisher
were soon bored.

"I can't see any people-folk," said
Bramble. "Let's do something."

"Like what?" said Berry and Wisher.

"Race you to the bridge!"
said Bracken.

"What if people-folk see us?"
said Fern.

"We'll RUN!" said the others.

"Stay where I can see you," said Mellow. "And don't get up to mischief!"

"Yes, Marr!" said the young rabbits.

Mellow watched them dash towards the river. Bracken led the way. He was faster than the rest. But as he approached the bridge, he heard a strange noise.

Tap, tap, tap!

Bracken stopped and the others piled into him.

"Ooops!"　　　　　*"Ow!"*

　　　　　　　　　　　　"Ouch!"

"Ooof!"

"Sssh!" said Bracken. "There's someone by the river. Listen!"

Tap, tap, tap!

"Parr was right," said Bramble. "People-folk are coming. There's one here already!"

"I don't like it," said Bracken.

"What's he doing?" said Berry.

"Whatever it is," said Fern, "let's go before he sees us."

"No," said Wisher. "Let's hide under the bridge and watch."

Fern wasn't happy, but she didn't want to go home alone. The five young rabbits squeezed under the wooden planks. There was just enough room for them to sit without being seen.

"Parr said people-folk put ducks in a box," said Fern. "Maybe those are for rabbits!"

"It's a bit small . . ." said Bramble.

"Fern could be right," said Wisher. "Parr said somebody put him in a cage. The box might be another way for people-folk to catch animals."

A movement in the water caught everyone's attention. A small animal was swimming across the river towards them. It was Violet Vole.

"Hello," said Violet. "What are you doing?"

Wisher told Violet everything they had seen and heard that day, and why they were watching the man with a box.

"Oh, my whiskers!" said Violet. "What a terrible tale! I must spread the news at

once." And off she went.

Just then, the rabbits heard their marr calling. They crept out from under the bridge and ran back to the burrow.

"Thank the stars you're safe!" cried Mellow. "Where were you? I've looked everywhere! I saw someone by the river. I thought you'd been . . . oh, never mind! Come along inside."

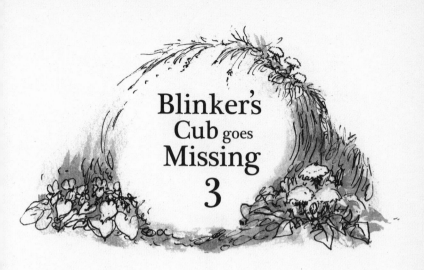

Blinker's Cub goes Missing
3

After her meeting with Wisher and the others, Violet Vole swam downriver. She couldn't wait to pass on every word of Wisher's shocking story. There was a lot to remember and Violet hoped she'd got everything right. The first friend she met was Hazel Heron who was fishing by the riverbank.

"Have you heard?" said Violet.
"Wisher says people-folk are taking over!
They want our homes, you see? I saw
one, or was it two, with my own eyes!
They're destroying Oak Wood. One tree
almost fell on Blinker Badger. He had
a very lucky escape. The crows are in a
flap about something . . . I've forgotten
why. They're in the big oak and making
a terrible noise.

Oh, and did I mention the boxes? Wisher says they're for catching animals. Barley saw some ducks in a box once, so she must be right."

"Oh, my beak and feathers!" said Hazel. "Things couldn't be any worse. Thank you, Violet."

Hazel flew away to tell someone, and the first friend she met was Daisy Duck.

"Wait till you hear this," said Hazel. "People-folk are taking over! Wisher says she saw some in the big oak and they're making a terrible noise!

The crows are in a flap, which is not surprising. Someone cut their trees in Oak Wood! Blinker saw everything with his own eyes. He tried to escape, but he was caught and put in a box with Barley."

"Quack, quack, quack!" said Daisy. "What a dreadful story! I must make sure my ducklings are safe."

Daisy paddled off. On the way to her ducklings, she met Sylvia Squirrel.

"Quack, quack, quack!" said Daisy. "Have you heard the news? We're in trouble! People folk are taking over. They plan to live in Oak Wood and . . . everywhere!

They've cut down all the trees, and made a big box to put us in. Blinker and the crows had a narrow escape, but poor Barley is shut up in a box!"

"Oh!" said Sylvia. "I must go and see Mellow at once."

To her surprise, Sylvia found Barley pacing up and down outside his burrow.

"I was worried about you," said Sylvia. "There are some funny stories going about. Daisy Duck told me . . ."

Barley listened while Sylvia told him what she'd heard.

"Some of it is just gossip," said Barley. "You know how stories get about. But most of it is true. Wisher, Bramble, Bracken, Berry and Fern did see someone by the bridge. And the crows saw what was happening in Oak Wood."

"Those noisy crows!" said Sylvia.
"I haven't had a moment's peace since
they arrived."

Mellow hopped over and joined them.
"We can hear the crows from here,"
she said.

"True," said Barley. "But they lost their
nests, remember? We must be nice to
them." Barley tugged his ear. "Oh dear,
as if we didn't have enough to worry
about with foxes and Burdock. Now we
have to watch out for people-folk too!"

Wisher had been nibbling grass
nearby and listening. She sat up, a
puzzled look on her face. Her ears
were tingling.

"What is it?" said Mellow.

"It's just a feeling," said Wisher.

"I think someone may be lost."

Blinker couldn't think what had
happened. The last time he'd looked, his
four cubs had been playing a game of
rough and tumble in a hollow by the sett.

Then, suddenly, Briar had vanished.
He was nowhere to be seen. Blinker left
his other three cubs at home with their
mother, then set off to look for Briar.

After searching Oak Wood, Blinker
decided he would need help from
his friends.

"I'll ask Barley to organise a search
party," he said.

As he got to the tunnel that went
under the Red Dragon's tracks, Blinker
stopped. He'd had a terrifying thought.
What if Briar had strayed on to the tracks!
What if the Dragon . . .

Blinker ran up the embankment and
stood by the iron rails. He looked both
ways down the line. There was no sign
of Briar, or the Red Dragon. He thought
about going through the tunnel, but
decided that from here it was quicker to
cross the tracks.

As Blinker was crossing the rails to the
far side, he realised he hadn't seen the
Red Dragon for some time.

He was used to seeing the Dragon
roaring along the valley in spring and
summer. Maybe, thought Blinker, the Red
Dragon sleeps in winter? But spring is in
the air. The Dragon will be back soon!

Blinker thought no more about it.
He was much too worried about Briar.
He ran down a grassy slope, then on to
the Longears' burrow.

Word spread quickly about the missing
badger cub. Violet Vole, Hazel Heron
and Sylvia Squirrel were sure Briar had
been captured by people-folk! There
were so many stories going around,
nothing would have surprised them. It
didn't take long for Barley and Blinker
to organise a search party. Soon, friends
were gathering at the tree stump, eager
to help.

Apart from Mellow and the five young rabbits, there were:

Parsley Mole,

Sylvia Squirrel,

Hazel Heron,

Violet Vole,

Daisy Duck,

Craggs and Clary Crow and . . .

all the noisy crows from the big oak!

Barley put everyone into groups and they tried to decide where to look for Blinker's cub. The crows couldn't agree where they should start and argued noisily.

Caw-caw-caw! Caw-caw-caw!

"Oh, do be quiet!" said Violet.

"I can't hear myself think!" said Daisy.

"You're giving me a headache," said Hazel.

Wisher's ears were tingling. Words were spinning round inside her head, but the crows were making such a noise she couldn't hear them properly. I must concentrate, thought Wisher. She moved to a quieter place to listen . . .

At last, the crows agreed.

"We'll fly over Oak Wood," said Chuff.

"We might spot Briar from the air," said Chaff.

"Good idea!" said their friends.

Chuff and Chaff and the other crows all took off together.

Caw-caw-caw! Caw-caw-caw!

"Peace at last!" said Barley, as he hopped towards the wooden bridge with Blinker and Sylvia.

"I've hardly had a wink of sleep since those crows arrived in the big oak," said Sylvia.

"But crows have sharp eyes," said Blinker. "We're lucky they're helping to search for Briar."

"Children are such a worry, aren't they?" said Sylvia. "You can't take your eyes off them for a minute before they're off and up to all sorts! I shouldn't be surprised if Briar hasn't been caught by people-folk."

Blinker looked horrified.

"Oh, don't say that!" he said.

Barley rolled his eyes.

Sometimes Sylvia didn't think before she spoke. Though after all the stories he'd heard lately, Barley wondered if this time she could be right.

The three animals walked along a path by the river, looking under every bush and behind every tree. Barley noticed a few changes to their otherwise familiar surroundings. He wasn't sure what to make of it.

"Hm!" he said. "Lots of new trees."

Blinker couldn't stop thinking about what Sylvia had said. Supposing people-folk had taken Briar? What would they do to him?

Suddenly, Blinker saw something lying on the ground. He thought Briar might be under there.

"Be careful!" said Sylvia. "It could be a trap."

Barley and Sylvia helped Blinker lift one end, and they peered underneath. But all they found was a small lizard.

"Sorry," said Blinker. "We didn't mean to disturb you."

They replaced the shelter and were
just setting off again, when they heard
a shout.

"Parr! Blinker! Sylvia!"

It was Wisher. She came running up to
them. Then she repeated the words she'd
heard in her head earlier:

"The badger cub is safe and sound,
You will find him undergroud!
He's hiding in a place you know –
To Blinker's Tunnel you must go!"

"The tunnel!" cried Blinker. "Why
didn't I think of it? Thank you, Wisher!"

Chuff and Chaff and the other crows had been circling above Oak Wood. They called and called Briar's name, hoping the cub would hear them:

Caw-caw-caw!

> *Briar! Briar! Briar!*

Briar did hear. He had been curled up near one end of the tunnel, too scared to move. He was cold and hungry, and wanted to go home. When Briar heard the crows, he suddenly found the courage to go outside . . .

"There he is!" cried Clary, her bright eyes shining with delight.

"Caw!" said Craggs. "The little cub is safe."

"We'll spread the good news," said Chuff and Chaff.

It wasn't long before Wisher, Barley, Blinker and Sylvia arrived.

"Parr!" cried Briar.

Blinker ran and gave him a cuddle.

"What happened?" he said. "I've been so worried."

"P-p-people-folk," said Briar. "I saw them coming. I thought they wanted to catch me. I was so frightened I ran away."

"You're safe now," said Blinker. "Wisher helped us find you."

"Thank you, Wisher," said Briar. He smiled at the crows. "Thank you, crows!"

"Pleased to help," said Chuff.

"Any time," said Chaff.

"Yes," cried all the other crows cheerfully. "Any time at all."

Caw-caw-caw! Caw-caw-caw!

By now, the whole search party had gathered at Blinker's Tunnel. Everyone cheered. Maybe the crows aren't so bad after all, they thought – even if they are noisy!

Parsley was admiring Blinker's Tunnel.

"It was the best place to hide," he told Blinker. "You can't beat a tunnel, eh?"

"Yes," said Blinker. "Come to think of it, this tunnel was built by people-folk. They did a fine job too! It's just the right size for badgers."

"Up the burrowers!" said Parsley.

Bramble, Bracken, Berry, Fern and Wisher pricked their ears. They had heard so many bad stories about people-folk it was a surprise to hear something good.

"So, sometimes people-folk . . . help animals?" said Wisher.

Barley thought for a moment. "I suppose they do," he said.

"It's very confusing," said Wisher.

Then they all went home.

Nature Trails
4

Down the line at the Ripple Valley Steam Railway Station, the cats, Florence and Skittles, were sitting next to the Booking Office stove. Florence had just finished washing her smooth black and white coat, and was inspecting her snowy white paws.

"Purrfect!" she said, when she was sure each one was spotless.

Skittles, a tabby with a smudgy black nose, thought Florence looked beautiful.

He gave his ear a quick
wash before settling down
for a snooze. He was just
getting comfortable when
the door opened and some
people came in.

"Uh-oh," said
Florence. "We weren't
expecting visitors. What's going on?"

Skittles sat up.

"I've no idea," he said. "Let's find out."

The cats recognised a few familiar
faces – George the station master, and
John the engineer, for example – but
there were a few strangers too. Some
were carrying notebooks, and there was
a man with a camera, taking pictures.
He took one of Florence and Skittles by
the stove.

George called for everyone's
attention. Florence and Skittles
listened carefully. They didn't want to
miss a thing!

"Thank you for coming," said George.
"As some of you know, conservation
work has been going on for several
weeks at Oak Wood and along the river."

"Conversation work?" said Skittles.
"What's that?"

"No, silly!" said Florence.
"Con-serv-ation. I think it means looking
after the environment."

"You know a lot
of big words," said
Skittles. "My head is
spinning already!"

George pointed to a large map on the wall and continued:

"The Ripple Valley Steam Railway owns this land. We want to protect it for wildlife, and allow visitors to enjoy this lovely part of the valley too. I'm pleased to announce that Oak Wood Nature Trails will be ready in time for the Easter holidays. So, not long to go! We are running a special train service to Oakwood Crossing to celebrate the opening!"

"Excellent," said one man.

"A great idea," said another.

George smiled. "Are there any questions?" he said.

A young woman holding a notebook raised her hand. George knew she was a reporter from the local newspaper.

"Could you tell us a little more about the work you've been doing?" she said.

"Of course," said George. "We've taken expert advice. We've put up nesting boxes for owls and other birds, and provided shelters for reptiles, such as grass snakes and lizards. They love to hide where it's dark and warm! We're trying to attract as many species of wildlife as possible . . ."

"Wildlife?" said Florence.

"You know," said Skittles. "Animals like, er, let me think . . . rabbits! I saw some rabbits once. They seemed quite friendly."

"Are all wild animals friendly?" said Florence.

"I'm not sure . . ." said Skittles.

"Some trees had to be cut," George was saying, "but only where necessary. I'm afraid our chainsaws made rather a lot of noise! But we've planted new trees to take their place."

"Thank you," said the young woman. "Is there any information for visitors about the plants and animals?"

"Yes," said George. "We've printed lots of leaflets!"

OAK WOOD

THERE ARE MANY WILD ANIMALS, BIRDS, TREES AND PLANTS IN OAKWOOD.

CARE MUST BE TAKEN TO AVOID DISTURBING THE INHABITANTS, OR DAMAGING THEIR HABITAT IN ANYWAY.

DOGS MUST BE KEPT ON A LEAD AT ALL TIMES.

OAK WOOD

THERE ARE MANY WILD ANIMALS, BIRDS, TREES AND PLANTS IN OAKWOOD.

CARE MUST BE TAKEN TO AVOID DISTURBING THE INHABITANTS, OR DAMAGING THEIR HABITAT IN ANYWAY.

DOGS MUST BE KEPT ON A LEAD AT ALL TIMES.

He held one up and read from it: "There are many wild animals, birds, trees and plants in Oak Wood. Care must be taken to avoid disturbing the woodland inhabitants, or damaging their habitat in any way. Dogs must be kept on leads at all times."

"Quite right!" said Florence.

There were no more questions and the meeting ended. Florence and Skittles curled up again, ready to go to sleep.

"Oak Wood Nature Trails sounds interesting," said Skittles. "Shall we go, Florence?"

"I don't know," said Florence.

"We might meet some unfriendly wild animals."

"I'll look after you," said Skittles sleepily. "I always do."

One sunny spring morning, the Big Day
arrived. Skittles and Florence liked the
way George had decorated The Station
with flags and coloured balloons.

The big, red steam engine, SPITFIRE
Number 47512, looked very smart – its
bright red paint gleaming in the sunshine.
John had cleaned the pipes and pistons,
and checked that all the parts were oiled
and working properly. The carriages
had been given a fresh coat of paint, and
their wooden seats cleaned and polished.
SPITFIRE stood by the platform, hissing
steam and ready to go.

The Booking Office was full of people
buying tickets, and excited children
running about. Florence had agreed
to go with Skittles to Oak Wood Nature
Trails. But now it was time, she wasn't
sure it was such a good idea.

The cats waited until all the carriages were full of passengers. Then they hopped aboard and hid under a seat.

"Phew!" said Skittles. "We made it."

"I'm nervous about those wild animals," said Florence. "I think I've changed my mind . . ."

Just then, George waved a green flag, and SPITFIRE gave a piercing whistle.

Whooo-Wheeep!

"Too late," said Skittles. "Here we go!"

The train gave a jolt and pulled away from the platform. Soon, it was rattling and clattering down the track at full speed, on its way to Oakwood Crossing.

Springtime Surprises
5

That day, Wisher woke early. Everyone else was still sleeping. She didn't want to wake them, so she crept along a tunnel and went up-burrow.

Wisher wrinkled her nose.

"Spring!" she said. "The meadow is full of sweet grass and wildflowers!"

Wisher nibbled a stalk of grass and thought about things that had happened recently.

Blinker's cub had gone missing. She
was pleased they'd found him quickly,
and the crows had been helpful too. At
least that meant Sylvia, Violet and the
other animals weren't quite so cross with
them about the noise they were making.

Then she thought about Craggs
and Clary. They had been very upset
at the thought of losing their home in the
big oak. They were looking forward to
having their first family.

Wisher tried to picture a nest full of baby crows, all crying at once.

"Even more noise!" she said.

Suddenly her ears began to tingle. She looked back at her burrow, but she couldn't see anyone. Everywhere was still and quiet, until . . .

Caw-caw-caw! Caw-caw-caw!

"The crows!" said Wisher. "Oh no! Something's wrong."

Wisher didn't stop to think. She ran to the big oak as fast as she could. She looked up into the tree, full of new green leaves. Wisher could see the crows. They were flapping their wings and crying at the tops of their beaks:

Caw-caw-caw! Caw-caw-caw!

Suddenly, Craggs and Clary flew out of the treetop into the sky. Wisher saw they were chasing another bird – a bigger bird. She gasped. Burdock the buzzard!

Caw-caw-caw!
Caw-caw-caw!

called Chuff and Chaff and all the other crows in alarm.

Wisher dived under a bush and crouched there, shaking. From her hiding place, she could see Craggs and Clary. She watched in fright as the crows attacked the buzzard.

Burdock soared higher, just out of reach, then dived. The crows swooped on either side, keeping pace with their enemy. Then Craggs tipped Burdock's wing with his own. It was enough to push the buzzard off course, and he flew away.

Wisher waited until she was sure Burdock had gone and crawled from under the bush. Craggs spotted her and flew down.

"Caw!" said Craggs. "Burdock was after our babies. We have four chicks!"

"Congratulations!" said Wisher. "I hope they'll be okay."

"What with Burdock and people-folk," said Craggs, "we'll have to keep our ears and eyes open for trouble."

"Good luck," said Wisher. "See you soon!"

Wisher said goodbye, then ran back to her burrow. It had been a surprising start to the day.

Wisher found her parr and marr outside with Bramble, Bracken, Berry and Fern. They were talking about the crows.

"They woke me up!" said Barley.

"Me too," said Mellow.

"Why do they have to make such a noise?" said Bramble.

"It was worse than ever this morning," said Bracken.

"I wonder what the fuss was about this time?" said Berry.

"Ooo!" said Fern. "Maybe they were attacked by people-folk . . ."

"Actually," said Wisher, "it was Burdock!" She described what had happened.

She had just finished when they heard a
piercing whistle.

Whooo-Wheeep!

"The Red Dragon!" cried the
young rabbits.

"He's back," said Barley. "I wonder
where he's been?"

From the Longears' burrow the rabbits
could just see the Dragon's tracks – a
straight line running between the River
Ripple and Oak Wood.

Everyone waited, expecting to see the monster racing along the valley, puffing clouds of smoke. Then they saw he had stopped at Oakwood Crossing.

Barley frowned. "Hm?" he said. "He doesn't usually stop there."

"Maybe something's wrong?" said Bramble. "I remember the Red Dragon did stop there once," said Bracken.

"Yes," said Berry. "The day he got stuck in the snow!"

"There's no snow today," said Fern. "So what's the matter?"

Wisher was only half-listening because her ears were tingling. She held her paws to her head.

"Sssh!" she said. "A voice is telling me something. It's strange. I can hardly hear it."

She repeated the message, pausing where she thought there were missing words.

"I whisper a song like the wind in your ear.
Tell your friends . . . to fear,
Folk . . . with hammer and saw –
Will . . . your homes forever more!"

"Oh, buttercups!" said Barley, tugging his ears. "Those terrible stories were true after all."

Just then, Bramble, Bracken, Berry and Fern pointed towards Oakwood Crossing and gave a shout:

"PEOPLE-FOLK!"

It was the moment they had all been dreading. The invasion had begun! They stared, wide-eyed with fear, as people-folk spread out along the riverbank and into Oak Wood.

"This is the end!" said Fern. "We're doomed for EVER!"

A group of anxious animals gathered at Barley's tree stump. They were all frightened, but everyone was determined to try to save their homes.

"Caw!" said Craggs. "If anyone comes near my nest, I'll peck them!"

"I've got sharp claws," said Blinker.

"I can bite," said Violet.

"I can scratch," said Sylvia.

Parsley blinked, wondering what he could do.

"I can dig," he said. "But I don't think it would help."

Barley paced up and down.

"I'm not sure ANYTHING would stop people-folk doing what they want to do," he said. "If only we knew what they were up to."

Wisher pointed to the wooden bridge.

"We could ask those cats," she said.

"They've just got off the Red Dragon!"

A Purrfect Arrangement
6

Florence and Skittles jumped down
from the carriage and went to explore.
Florence followed Skittles along a path
to the river.

"We mustn't go too far," said Florence.
"We don't want to miss the train home."

"Don't worry," said Skittles. "I know
the Timetable. There'll be plenty of time
to look around before the whistle goes.
Let's sit by the bridge. If we're lucky, we
may see some fish!"

"Well, I hope we don't meet any wild animals," said Florence, nervously.

What she saw next made her fur stand on end.

"Help!" cried Florence. "We'll be eaten alive!"

"It's all right," said Skittles. "Look. The little white rabbit is waving to us."

A few moments later, they all met on the wooden bridge.

"Hello," said Wisher. "I'm Wisher. This is my parr, Barley Longears."

"I'm Skittles," said Skittles. "We live at the railway Station."

"I'm Florence," said Florence. She eyed the wild animals suspiciously.

Barley thought the cats were very brave to ride on the Red Dragon.

"What's going on?" he said. "Why are people-folk here?"

"Have they come to take our homes?" said Wisher.

Florence and Skittles couldn't believe their ears. "No!" said Skittles. "Whatever made you think that?"

"Quite the opposite," said Florence. "These people love wild animals. They'd do anything to help you."

"WHAT!" said everyone.

"It's like this . . ." said Florence.

"We'll try to explain . . ." said Skittles.

The cats told them everything they knew about Oak Wood Nature Trails, and how the railway people were working to protect the woods and riverbank. By the time Florence and Skittles had finished, everyone was speechless. At last, Barley spoke:

"Well," he said, "that's very reassuring."

"Yes," said Florence. "It's an understanding between animals and people, you see? You learn to share the place you live with people-folk. In return, they'll save your homes and try not to disturb you. It's a Purrfect Arrangement!"

Chuff and Chaff and the other crows
were delighted and already making plans.

"We're going back to Oak Wood to
build new nests!" said Chuff.

"The big oak was getting a bit
crowded," said Craggs and Clary.

"Caw! Caw! Caw!" said the
other crows.

"I can't wait!" said Sylvia Squirrel.

"What a relief," said Violet Vole.

"I'll say!" said Parsley.

"About time too," said Hazel Heron.

"Hm?" said Blinker to the crows. "Just try and keep the noise down . . . please!"

"We will!" said the cheeky crows.

Caw-caw-caw! Caw-caw-caw!

There were cheers all round. Then above the noise of all the animals, there came a shrill whistle.

Whooo-Wheeep!

"Time to go," said Skittles.

Florence and Skittles said goodbye to their new friends and hurried away.

Wisher saw them jump aboard the Red Dragon just in time.

That night, as Wisher settled down to sleep, she heard the message again. Only this time, there were no missing words:

"I whisper a song like the wind in your ear.
Tell your friends they have nothing to fear,
Folk who come with hammer and saw –
Will save your homes forever more!"

Wisher repeated the message when Mellow came to kiss her goodnight. "I don't understand, Marr," she said. "Why didn't I hear it properly the first time?"

Mellow smiled. "Sometimes we're afraid of things for no reason," she said. "We imagine the worst when there's nothing to fear. We'll always have real enemies like Burdock to worry about. But if we're sensible rabbits, we shall live here for a very long time."

Wisher snuggled happily in her nest. She was sure Marr was right. Then she fell fast asleep.

Acknowledgements

Inspiration for *The Railway Rabbits* came from the view from my window. The Launceston Steam Railway runs along the Kensey river valley, North Cornwall, linking the historic town of Launceston at one end of the line with the hamlet of Newmills at the other. My thanks to Kay and Nigel Bowman for their wonderful railway, Richard and Sandra Ball at New Mills Farm Park – and to all the rabbits in between.

Georgie Adams